Sticky Green Noses Help Save The Brook

Stacey Giaquinto

Sticky Green Noses Help Save The Brook
All Rights Reserved.
Copyright © 2016 Stacey Giaquinto
v2.0

Illustrated by: Richa Kinra.
Illustrations © 2016 Outskirts Press, Inc. All rights reserved - used with permission.

Outskirts Press, Inc.
http://www.outskirtspress.com

ISBN: 978-1-4787-6123-5

Outskirts Press and the "OP" logo are trademarks belonging to Outskirts Press, Inc.

PRINTED IN THE UNITED STATES OF AMERICA

DENVER, COLORADO

Kids *can* make a difference! :) *[signature]*

This Book Belongs to:

_____

There is a water brook at the end of our Mimi's street. My brother and I play there; it's mostly kind of neat. We go for walks around the brook on the grass which grows beside it. One day we found a bullfrog, and my brother tried to ride it.

Another time we collected the biggest, roundest rocks. We tossed them into the water to make great, humungous plops.

We visited the brook on many, many days...until one time we realized an awful scary craze. We noticed that the water is not the only thing that flows. The stinky smell of garbage was flowing right up into our nose!

There were candy wrappers, soda cans, newspapers and more junk, all kinds of empty containers, broken glass, the tail of a skunk, a ball used for bowling, a notebook, plastic bags, many, many pieces of ripped up dirty rags, a CD, a piece of string, a plate, a plastic fork, a shoelace, a trash can lid, and a floating bottle cork.

As we walked around the brook we hollered, "Hey, this place is not at all clean. The people who put their garbage in there are being horribly mean!"

"Don't these people know that our Earth is a precious place? The land that we all live upon, we should not deface!"

What can we do to help clean the brook and rid the raunchy smell? My brother and I both agreed we needed to go and tell. Before we left, two maple seeds spiraled down right near our toes. We picked them up, peeled them back, and stuck them on our nose.

Perhaps the seeds would shoo away the smell of trash that made an offensive reek. Then we decided to go and get some help, the neighbors we would seek. Tell our Mimi and our friends—and the entire neighborhood—to bring a bunch of trash cans so we can make the brook look like it should.

Our Mimi wondered why we had the seeds stuck onto our nose. My brother and I quickly told her just how our story goes. I said, "You know the brook right down the street where my brother and I play? Well, when we looked down into the water, we noticed that there was garbage on display." Then my brother told her about the variety of trash. He asked, "How can all these people be so very crass? There were candy wrappers, soda cans, newspapers, and more junk, all kinds of empty containers, broken glass, the tail of a skunk, a ball used for bowling, a notebook, plastic bags, many, many pieces of ripped up dirty rags, a CD, a piece of string, a plate, a plastic fork, a shoelace, a trash can lid, and a floating bottle cork!"

As we finished telling our Mimi about the polluted brook, on her face she wore a rather disgruntled look. We quickly rounded up the neighbors and explained the dirty scene. Then we all set out to make a difference and make our Earth look clean.

We gathered some supplies, like bags and barrels and rakes. We all began to shout, "There's a difference we can make!"

As we walked along the brook, we picked up more maple seeds. We all stuck them on our noses and began our modest deeds. The seeds plugged up our nostrils, so the rotten smell wouldn't be so strong. Now it was time to clean up after all those people who treated our Earth so wrong.

We strolled along the brook with pride, our noses bright and green, and picked up every bit of garbage after those who treat Mother Nature so mean.

Next time you see some trash on the street or along the beach, remember there is a lesson to be learned and your job is to make sure you teach. Teach all the people who think it's OK to throw their garbage on the ground. Teach them not to litter and please recycle...the difference will be profound!

CPSIA information can be obtained at www.ICGtesting.com
Printed in the USA
BVIW12n2034131016
464874BV00001B/1